HIGH
DRAMA

WOODLAND HIGH SCHOOL
800 N. MOSELEY DRIVE
STOCKBRIDGE, GA 30281
(770) 389-2784

SUSPENDED

HIGH DRAMA

Brandon Terrell

MINNEAPOLIS

Darby Creek
A division of Lerner Publishing Group, Inc.
241 First Avenue North
Minneapolis, MN 55401 USA

For reading levels and more information, look up this title at
www.lernerbooks.com.

Front cover: © Jon Feingersh Photography/Getty Images (teen girl); Cover and interior: © iStockphoto.com/Sorapop (ripped paper).

Main body text set in Janson Text LT Std 12/17.5.
Typeface provided by Adobe Systems.

Library of Congress Cataloging-in-Publication Data

Terrell, Brandon, 1978–
    High drama / Brandon Terrell.
        pages cm
    Summary: After seeing her best friend, Kat, kissing another girl, Dessa keeps the secret but her anger over Kat not confiding in her causes trouble.
    ISBN 978-1-4677-5710-2 (lb : alk. paper)
    ISBN 978-1-4677-8097-1 (pb : alk. paper)
    ISBN 978-1-4677-8826-7 (eb pdf)
    [1. Best friends—Fiction. 2. Friendship—Fiction. 3. High schools—Fiction. 4. Schools—Fiction. 5. Secrets—Fiction. 6. Lesbians—Fiction. 7. Theater—Fiction.] I. Title.
PZ7.T273Hig 2015
[Fic]—dc23   2014041435

Manufactured in the United States of America
1 – SB – 7/15/15

CHAPTER ONE

Bzzzt-bzzzt. Bzzzt-bzzzt.

In the darkness of Mr. Jacoby's Earth Science class, I clawed at my back pocket. I needed to reach my phone before it vibrated again. It was against the rules to have a phone in class. If Mr. Jacoby caught me, he'd confiscate the thing, and I wouldn't see it until the end of the week.

Which, let's face it, is basically the end of time itself when you don't have a phone.

I found it, clicked it off. A couple of kids nearby turned to look at me, but nobody really gave a crap.

"Is everything all right, Dessa?" Mr. Jacoby's nasally voice chirped over the video he was making us watch. It played on an old television perched on an audio-video cart that looked like it might topple over and crush an unsuspecting kid. On the screen, a narrator droned on about the various layers of the earth's crust.

Riveting stuff.

"Everything's cool, Mr. J," I answered in a too-perky voice. Mr. Jacoby hated when people called him that.

He went back to watching the video, eyes fixed on the screen like he hadn't seen the same thing during the first two periods of the morning.

Who called me?

Keeping my eyes on Mr. Jacoby, I slid the phone out of my pocket. As I did, it vibrated again, and my screen blazed bright in the darkness of the classroom. I pressed the phone against my chest. This time, my actions didn't warrant a glance from my middle-aged, balding science teacher.

I waited a moment longer to be sure, then snuck a glance at my screen. The call I'd missed a minute ago was from my best friend, Kat. She'd also just sent me a text.

SOMETHING 2 TALK ABOUT, it read. CUT CLASS. MEET ME @ THE USUAL SPOT IN 15.

My nose wrinkled in confusion. Kat and I were about as close as two friends could be, yet I had zero clues what she could be talking about. And just like that, my trembling hands could hardly hold onto my phone.

It must be mega-important if it can't wait until after school, I thought as I shoved the phone back into my pocket. I began to nervously twist the streak of blue in my black hair. Kat and I had dyed it a couple of months back. She'd since gone back to being blonde; I'd decided to keep my rebellious streak.

I have to get out of here.

"Mr. J?" I hissed, raising my hand. "Yo! Mr. J!?"

Mr. Jacoby's eyes rolled at the second mention of his nickname. "Yes, Miss Kingston?"

"I gotta run to the bathroom." And then I lobbed out the two words that made every male teacher at Brookstone High squirm. "Girl stuff."

As expected, Mr. Jacoby nodded at the door. "Of course, of course," he mumbled.

I snatched my backpack off the floor, slung it over one shoulder, and wove through desks to the door.

The ancient, brick halls of Brookstone High were quiet. Rows of baby blue lockers, battered and dented after years of use and misuse, lined the corridor. I passed a number of classrooms closed off by thick wooden doors.

The "usual spot" Kat had talked about in her text was a patch of trees back behind the school, out beyond the track and football field. A tiny path in the woods led to an outcropping of rocks that clung to the shadows no matter the time of day.

Students had used the rocks while cutting class for years. Kat and I started hanging out there last spring, when her parents were going through a messy divorce and she needed a place to cry and curse and talk to someone whose only job was to shut up and listen.

We understood each other, Kat and I. We didn't keep secrets, and we didn't lie to one another.

I rounded a corner on the south side of the building and began to head toward the cafeteria. That's when I spied Ms. Updahl walking my way. She was ancient, a crusty relic of a teacher. If I didn't have her for English class in the afternoon, I'd have probably just assumed she was a ghost forced to haunt the halls of Brookstone for eternity, scowling and shushing students. Thankfully, there was a bathroom on my right. I ducked inside until I heard Ms. Updahl's high-heeled boots pass.

During the school day, most of the heavy metal doors are locked. No one gets in, no one sneaks out. There are, of course, a few workarounds. And I know them all. The easiest one is here on the south side, past the auditorium and the stage entrance and the dressing rooms. It's a door the janitors use on-and-off all day, mostly in the afternoon, because there's a line of gigantic dumpsters just outside. This is where the remainder of our— insert grotesque adjective here—leftovers from lunch are deposited every day.

You have to be kind of careful sneaking out this door, though. Sometimes Ron, the head janitor, is just hanging out. He'll be sneaking a smoke and reading a magazine. Usually *Lowrider* or *Hot Rod*.

This time, though, the gods were with me.

As I passed the backstage area of the auditorium, I noticed a crack in the auditorium doorway. There was a light on, fairly bright, so I could only assume it was one of the spotlights over the stage. A pink poster had been taped to the black metal door. The design had flowing black letters written in calligraphy inside the shape of a scroll. *Romeo & Juliet*, it read. The ampersand between the star-crossed lovers' names was all big and swirling.

"Art class suck-up," I whispered.

I was about to continue on my way when I heard voices coming from inside the auditorium.

"But she's your best friend," the first voice said. It was a girl, but I didn't recognize the voice.

". . . really don't think it's a good idea," the second person countered. I placed this voice right away.

"Kat?" I whispered.

I was more confused than ever. What was Kat doing in the auditorium? Usually we wouldn't be caught dead in there.

I looked both ways to make sure I was still flying solo in the hall. Then I pushed open the door and silently entered the backstage area.

It was dark and draped in shadows, with the only light coming from the main spotlight. I almost called out Kat's name as I wandered around backstage. But for some reason, I didn't.

"Just . . . just do whatever you want," the first voice said. There was a slight hitch at the end, like she was about to cry.

I couldn't see Kat and whoever it was she was talking to. Half-built sets—fake rock walls and castles built out of plywood sheets and 2x4s—blocked my view. The stage's enormous purple velour curtain was open, bunched up at both sides of the stage.

I felt weird, creeping up on my best friend. It almost made me want to hightail it out of there before I fell through a trap door in the stage or something.

Almost.

"Don't be like that, Arwen," Kat said.

Be like what?

Again, I opened my mouth.

Again, I remained silent.

I pushed aside part of the curtain and saw Kat. She was standing center stage, the spotlight from above casting her in its glow, dust particles swirling about her. She wore her favorite black leather coat and combat boots, and her blonde hair was bathed in angelic light.

The girl standing in front of her was Arwen McKenzie. I had kinda put two-and-two together when I heard Kat say her name a second ago. Not too many Arwens loitering the halls of Brookstone High. Anyway, Arwen was standing with a large red binder hugged tight against her chest. She sniffled, then wiped her cheek with one sleeve of her oversized sweatshirt.

"Look," Kat said, placing a hand on her hip. It was her 'I'm annoyed' motion. I'd seen it too many times to count. "I gotta run. She's probably waiting for me."

"Yeah," Arwen said. "Sure. Whatever."

And then, before I could step out and ask what in the name of Billy Shakespeare was going on, Kat stepped forward, placed her hands on Arwen's shoulders, and kissed her.

CHAPTER TWO

I couldn't believe my eyes.

Kat, the yin to my yang, the PB to my J, was kissing a girl.

I didn't even think she swung that way. Sure, she'd never really had a serious boyfriend, but there had been boys. Like Luke Best, who she dated for a while when I was with Luke's friend, Coen Marsh. But I never thought . . .

It wasn't until they parted that I realized I was eavesdropping on a very private moment. And it clicked that this, *this right in front of me*, was what Kat wanted to talk about.

And so I backtracked before either of the

girls noticed me. I followed the same path through the backstage area, making sure not to trip over anything or have my boots scuff the wooden floor, which was coated in black paint for some reason.

Then I was out the door, heading to the school exit just as fast as I could go. I wanted to be waiting in the woods for Kat, ready to talk and lend an ear or a shoulder. I didn't care who she loved or dated, boy or girl or slimy green alien from the planet Korbos VII. If she was happy, I was happy. Still, this was a huge deal. Life defining. If she was going to tell me, then I was going to let her tell me and pretend that I hadn't seen a thing.

It was sunny and cool outside, but not cold. Fall had taken root, but winter had yet to dig its icy grip into us. Nobody was outside by the dumpsters, so I dashed across the stretch of parking lot and toward the wooded area nearby. In the distance, I could hear one of the morning gym classes out on the track.

In the shade of the trees, the morning wind was colder. I pulled my flannel from my backpack and slipped it on. I glanced back over my shoulder. No sign of Kat yet.

When I reached the outcropping of rocks, I tossed my pack on the nearest one and sat down. My breath was ragged, and I realized I'd probably moved faster than I'd ever moved in gym class. The rocky surface beneath my butt was cold, and a chill passed through me.

Kat came walking down the path a couple of minutes later. I'd calmed a bit by then but still took a deep breath to settle my nerves. Why was I nervous? She was the one with the news, not me.

She moved down the path, head lowered, watching her feet with every step. She looked far more vulnerable than I'd ever seen her before. I could practically see the weight on her shoulders, and I wanted nothing more than to lift it right off her and cast it aside.

"Hey, Kit-Kat!" I tried to sound upbeat

but could hear a waver in my voice that wasn't usually there.

She looked up, gave me a half-hearted smile. "Oh, good," she said. "You got my text."

"Of course. Mr. J's pretty invested in his lame rock movie. Doubt he'll even remember I left. So . . . what's up?"

Kat leaned against a nearby boulder, where splinters of light cut through the trees and danced in her golden hair. Whereas I'd shed all of my childish looks, Kat still had a bit of baby fat in her cheeks, and her ears stuck out just a bit farther than normal. As a kid, I remember her trying to use loops of Scotch tape to try to pin her oversized ears back against her head. Now she just made sure her hair was long enough to cover them at all times.

She bit her lip—another nervous tic she'd had for years. "Nothing. Well, something, I guess. I don't know." Her voice trailed off.

"Everything all right?" My mind flashed to the beautiful image of Kat and Arwen in the spotlight. Everything seemed all right in that moment.

Kat nodded. "I just . . . well, I've been thinking a lot about something, and I wanted to run it by you."

"Okay."

This is it, I thought. I felt myself inching forward on the rock, near to the point of falling off.

"Well, it's just that . . ." she hesitated, and I held back from pushing her onward. Then she sighed, reached into her pocket, and removed a piece of folded, pink paper. She held it out to me. "Here."

I stared at the slip of paper, unmoving.

"Take it," she said, waggling it in front of me.

I did. Unfolded it. Stared at it. It was a flyer for *Romeo & Juliet* in the same silly font as the poster on the auditorium door. "What is this for?" I asked.

"Read it."

I scanned the paper. Opening night was just over three weeks away. Underneath the performance dates was a plea for help in bold black letters. "Set construction help needed," I read aloud. "Handy with a hammer? Great at wielding a paintbrush? Put those skills to work! Find William Tuttle in the halls and tell him you're game."

I don't know why, but I really wasn't piecing things together. Though I could tell Kat wasn't going to tell me about Arwen. At least, not yet.

Kat plucked a fallen leaf off the rock ledge where I sat. It was orange and brittle and crumbled at her touch. "I thought it'd maybe, I don't know, be kind of cool to help out," she said.

"Help out the theater geeks?"

"Yeah." Kat was not the type to step up and help out. She liked to stand back and let things happen.

And then, as before, it all slid into place. She didn't care so much about Shakespeare or the rest of the club or extracurriculars. She

wanted to be close to Arwen. And she didn't
want anyone to know why.

Not even me.

And I think that's why I suddenly grew
mad. This was me. *Me.* The person she'd come
to when her family had been torn apart like a
ship in a raging storm. The person she talked
to at three in the morning on the phone, when
there was more silence than speaking, because
we really had nothing more to discuss. The
person who saved her from drowning at Spring
Lake Park when we were ten and she didn't
know how to swim but dove into the deep end
anyway because she wanted to impress me.

*This is me, Kat. So why aren't you telling me
the truth?*

I jumped down from the rock. "This is
what you made me cut class for?" I asked,
holding up the flyer.

"Yeah," she answered, more breath than voice.

I shoved the flyer back at her. It crumpled
with the force. "Cool," I said. "Go ahead.

You don't need my permission to 'wield a paintbrush' with the Dork Squad."

"But . . . I thought maybe we could both do it."

I was a pot about to boil over. "No. And by the way, I—"

Saw you kissing Arwen McKenzie in the auditorium was the end of that sentence, but it died on my lips when I saw the hurt and bewilderment in Kat's eyes. She didn't deserve my anger. And she certainly didn't deserve what I was about to say.

"Forget about it," I said instead. "I'll see you around."

And I left her by the rocks, holding the crumpled up flyer to her chest as I trudged back through the woods, into the sunlight, and back toward Mr. J and his movie about rocks.

CHAPTER THREE

I didn't talk to Kat for the rest of the week.
We saw each other, though. Mrs. Engel's
Art class, second period. Mr. Hoffman's
Geography class, sixth period. We sat rows
away from each other but worlds apart. At
lunch, instead of eating with Kat in our usual
place, I would sit at a table by myself or with a
group of skateboarders Kat and I chilled with
sometimes. They weren't close friends, but
they didn't care if I tagged along.

I knew that I was angry at Kat, but I
was still struggling with why. She was going
through a lot, and I should totally have had her

back during it. But it really hurt my feelings that she hadn't trusted me. And, if I really wanted to be truthful, I was afraid that she'd found someone to replace me. Not like *that*, of course. Replaced by someone who understood her better.

So I kept my distance.

There were no texts or calls from her. Of course, I didn't try calling or texting her, either, so all was fair.

On day five, as the final bell rang and I wound my way back toward my locker, I ran into Grady Neelan in the hall. Grady was short and stocky, his wild hair crammed into a beanie. He already had his skateboard tucked between his backpack and he was making a mad dash for the door.

"Hey, Grady," I said, walking alongside him.

"Yo, Dess," he said in his gravelly monotone. No spikes in Grady's emotions. I couldn't tell if he was glad that he'd run into me or annoyed.

"You guys hitting Union?" I asked. Union Skatepark was located down near the rail yard. I don't know why I asked, though. I already knew the answer.

"You know it." We'd reached the end of the hall, where it split in a *T*. My locker was to the right. The school exit and the sweet freedom it offered were to the left. "Coming with us?" he asked.

I smiled and nodded. "You know it."

He dashed off without another word.

On my way out of the school, I took a detour and walked past the auditorium. Two sets of red double doors were set into the concrete walls, one for the lower-level seats and one for the balcony. Both were propped open, and I nearly turned back and went another way. I didn't want anybody to see me. Voices drifted out of the auditorium, and I could hear the sound of hammering and the whirring of a drill. Light music filtered from the auditorium speakers.

I didn't break my stride, just turned
and peered in through the door as I passed.
I briefly caught sight of the stage and of
the group of kids working on a castle set.
Tapestries were being painted on one wall. An
ornate frame was being hung on another.

Kat was there, standing near the wall,
paintbrush in hand.

I couldn't tell if she was happy or not.

Seeing her made my heart hurt a little.

 * * *

Union Skatepark wasn't much to look at. It was
basically a hollowed-out abandoned warehouse
where someone had constructed a bunch of
ramps and stuff. Black metal pulsed through
the warehouse, echoed off the walls, vibrated
in my chest. It was actually kind of nauseating.
I immediately wanted to turn back around
and leave. Then I saw Grady and a couple of
other skaters in a tattered booth, their arms
gesturing wildly as they tried to impress one

another with their boarding exploits.

Grady saw me approach, nodded his head. Another skater, Ramona, turned in her seat. She was wearing an *Akira* T-shirt and a ball cap pulled low over her hair. "Where's your deck, Dessa?" she asked. She had to shout to be heard over the music. She asked me this every time I showed up at Union to hang, even though she knew I didn't own a skateboard.

I've only set foot on a board once, and it didn't end well for me. I still had a tiny scar on my right elbow where I'd whacked the cement ledge surrounding the fountain in Brookstone Park.

I flipped Ramona a one-finger salute.

"Anybody wanna hit the half-pipe?" Grady asked, not even looking in my direction even though I *just* talked to him back at school.

"Let's do it." Ramona stood on the booth, looking like a gymnast as she dismounted onto the cement floor. She kicked her deck up into her hand. "Kick back and enjoy the show, D," she said to me. Then she brushed past me and rode out to the ramp. Grady and the others followed.

So I sat in a booth, all by myself. I watched as the crew of skaters practiced their moves. They landed some, bailed on others. Vic Lewis, a tall, dreadlocked dude with a video camera and a booming laugh, recorded them as they flipped their boards in the air or slammed their knees on the wooden ramps. I bought myself a fountain soda large enough to swim inside. I tried not to let the pulsing music get to me.

Most of all, I wondered why I was even there in the first place.

My mind was on Kat the whole time.

I couldn't stop thinking of her, working alongside a new group of friends. Did they know? Did anyone know, other than Arwen?

"This is so dumb," I said to myself, shaking my head and standing. I was sitting around, insanely bored, being a selfish little brat and hanging out with people I didn't even care about.

And so I left Union in my wake, not turning back. Nobody saw me leave.

* * *

The walk back to the school took about thirty minutes. By the time I reached the door by the dumpsters, the sun had dipped low in the sky and most of the people in town were probably sitting down to dinner with their families. I didn't know if the drama dorks were even at school anymore, but I wanted to check anyway.

I'd tried texting Kat on my way, but I hadn't gotten an answer.

As I approached, I noticed the door had been propped open with a cement block. Pieces of large poster board and debris jutted out of an open dumpster. One of the theater dorks, a short, stocky kid, was chucking what looked like a fake boulder made out of Styrofoam into it. The sight of it was actually pretty comical.

The kid turned to face me. He had thick glasses and close-cropped black hair. I recognized him from the halls, but I didn't know his name. I was pretty sure he was a freshman. Flecks of white paint coated his shirt, hands, and arms.

"Greetings and salutations," he said.

"What's up?" I answered.

He shrugged and said with a smirk, "Another day toiling for the Capulets."

I had no idea what he was talking about.

"I'm Quan, bee-tee-double-u," he said.

"Dessa."

"I know. You're Kat Beckford's friend, right? Dessa?"

"Yeah."

"Kat's crazy cool."

Quan held the door open for me, which was strange. Who does that? Well, Quan the Freshman, apparently. "After you, m'lady," he said.

I was a little weirded out, but considering

the complete apathy that had greeted me at Union Park, a little bit of weird was totally fine.

I walked through the same backstage door I'd used not even a week ago, when I'd accidentally stumbled onto Kat's secret. Quan was behind me, humming a tune and snapping his fingers.

The backstage area was still dark. Instead of music wafting through the speakers, I heard booming voices amplified through the empty auditorium.

"Hark!" a male voice called. "What light through yonder window breaks?"

"They're rehearsing Act Two right now," Quan whispered from behind me. "Kat's stage left. We're painting the Capulet castle interior. Follow me."

As the actors on stage continued their performance, Quan led me behind the framework for the set being used. I could see the actress playing Juliet standing on a ledge up above. I didn't know much about *Romeo &*

Juliet, aside from seeing the DiCaprio movie on TV once when Kat and I were bored and just wanted to watch eye candy. I recognized this scene, though. It's the one where Romeo wishes to be a glove or something.

A work area had been set up on the opposite side of the backstage area. A spotlight on the floor cast a striking glow on a set piece where three other people stood on ladders or knelt on the floor with paintbrushes.

I spied Arwen near the curtain, her eyes fixed on the actors on stage. Her hefty binder was open in her hands. She'd positioned a large pair of headphones with a mouthpiece on her head. She followed along with the actors, one finger tracing the script page in her binder. She glanced up at the lights, cupped her hand over the mic, and whispered something. A second later, the lights dimmed just a bit.

Kat was on one of the ladders, her back turned to me. I waited silently while Quan walked up and waved his arms at her. She looked down, then over, then saw me.

Her eyes lit up.

She dropped her paintbrush into a bucket perched precariously on the ladder's ledge, then climbed down. She almost fell but leapt from the last rung.

"Dessa!" she whisper-shouted. A few of the other kids turned to look at us. Out of the corner of my eye, I saw Arwen's gaze leave the stage to focus on me and Kat for a moment.

We hugged, and it was like all the pain and the anger washed away. It was just what I needed.

"I'm so glad you're here," Kat said. "I don't even know why we were fighting in the first place."

I do.

"Me neither," I said with a smile.

Our hug lasted a bit longer than hugs usually do, but neither of us cared. Then Kat drew back and held me at arm's length. "You're gonna have fun, I promise," she said.

I looked around. "Where do I start?"

Quan stepped up and handed me a paintbrush, like he had it ready and knew exactly what I was going to say. "M'lady."

"Uh, thanks," I said.

Then, with a grin beaming on her face, Kat explained what she and the others were painting. I hung my backpack on a hook near a line of ropes and sandbags, rolled up my sleeves, and got to work.

CHAPTER FOUR

Last winter, the drama club put on a
performance of a musical called *Fiddler on the
Roof.* I didn't see the play. Kat and I had better
things to do with our nights, like sneak out of
her dad's place to go party with Coen, Luke,
and a bunch of seniors. But one morning,
we all got out of first period to go down to
the auditorium to watch a scene. Mr. Baker,
the advanced English teacher and the play's
director, had introduced the performance. The
curtains parted, and what looked like a poor
village appeared.

The theater geeks hopped and danced and

spun around and sang, all while wearing thick woolen clothes lined with fur and hats with fur flaps. The whole time I was watching, the only thing I could think was . . .

"They look so hot and sweaty under the lights."

"I know, right?" Kat whispered from beside me. "The short one looks like he's going to pass out."

"God, I hope he doesn't keel over and fall off the stage," I said, snickering.

I thought about that morning as I stood backstage, paintbrush in hand, watching the two actors playing Romeo and Juliet. They faced each other center stage, about thirty feet from me, holding hands and staring deeply into one another's eyes. The boy playing Romeo was William Tuttle. Everyone knew Will. Class president, debate team captain, a voice for the students. Even the students who didn't care, like me and Kat. Tall and lean, Will's coffee-colored skin glistened under the harsh spotlights. Juliet was played by Maisie Bishop, a waif of a girl whose flowing, layered clothes made her look like she already wore a costume.

I found myself enamored as I watched them move about the stage, interacting with the other actors, reading from little pink script books they had secreted in their back pockets. I couldn't even fathom what it would be like to act, to pretend to be someone you're not in front of seats filled with parents, grandparents, siblings, friends, and strangers.

This was also what made me extremely uncomfortable about the whole scenario. Like, I was afraid someone was going to mistake me for a background actor. They'd slap an ill-fitting corset on me and make me stand up on stage in the blazing lights. With my luck, I'd pass out and fall into the seats, like Kat thought the little dude from *Fiddler* was going to do.

"These violent delights have violent ends," one of the other actors said to William, while Maisie waited in the wings to make her entrance. She rushed to William and took his hands. They looked comical. He was so tall and dark, and she was so . . . well, not.

The voice of Mr. Baker boomed from somewhere in the darkened seats. "All right. Thus ends Act Two. House lights to full."

William and Maisie let out a breath in unison, their shoulders deflating. "That was *so* good," William said.

"You've really got the rhythms down," Maisie told him.

From behind me, Arwen quietly said, "Please bring up the house, Heidi" into her mic.

The lights over the auditorium seats slowly turned on. Mr. Baker sat in the second row, taking notes in his wool coat and barely-tied tie. One light gleamed off his bald head. I didn't have him as a teacher but I walked by his class every day.

"Great work today, all," Mr. Baker said, closing his notebook and standing. He adjusted his coat. "Let's remember for tomorrow, this is the highest moment of joy for our star-crossed lovers. Though their love is a secret, they are beyond happy. They do not know that it will all come crashing down soon enough."

"Typical teenage love," William joked. "Am I right?"

His cast mates laughed. Mr. Baker smiled. "Precisely, Mr. Tuttle." He made a shooing motion with both hands. "That's all," he said. "Begone."

I hadn't been at my work space too long and hadn't made much damage, so Kat and I didn't have too much trouble cleaning up. As we did, Quan buzzed about, directing us where to place our dirty brushes and cans of paint. Kat and I carried our things back to a sink area. As we did, Arwen rushed out from behind the curtain, nearly colliding with Kat.

"Oh," she said. "Sorry."

"No problem," Kat said, like she'd never even spoken to Arwen before. Their eyes didn't linger on one another. There was no indication that they even knew each other's names. Arwen went on her way, and Kat continued to follow me back toward the sink.

I stacked my can of paint near an open cabinet containing a bunch of supplies. "She seems nice," I said.

"Who?" Kat asked. "Arwen?"

"Is that her name?"

"Yeah." Kat dropped her brush into the sink, which was half-filled with hot, soapy water.

And that was it.

No elaboration or anything.

I added my brush to the mix, then followed Kat back to the stage area.

The cast had gathered in the front couple of rows of red auditorium seats. Many of them shrugged on their coats and slung backpacks on their shoulders. Will Tuttle stood in the center of them all, as usual.

"Well, I'll be," he said, looking up as

Kat and I reached the edge of the stage. He shielded his eyes against the glare of the spotlight still beaming down on us. "Dessa Kingston, is that really you?"

"Hey, Will." Will and I had known each other since elementary school, but we rarely spoke. Different circles. I knew how much he hated to be called anything but William.

And, right on cue . . .

"Huh-uh," he said. "It's *William*, sweetie. Not Will. Not Bill. Not even will.i.am." He shook his arms at his sides.

I smirked. "Sure thing . . . William."

"Welcome to the DC-ers," he said.

"The what?" I asked.

"DC-ers. Drama Club. I can draw a diagram if you need it." He smiled, and I realized that he wasn't being sarcastic or anything. He was joking around.

I wasn't used to joking around.

"I'm good," I said. "I've seen your work in art class."

"Zing," Quan piped in from behind me.

"Some of us are going over to Pizza Palace," Maisie said, drinking from a flower-patterned water bottle. "You two wanna join us?"

I looked at Kat. I just wanted to go home, maybe eat a bowl of cereal while ignoring my parents and my two brothers, Isaac and Beckett.

I could see in Kat's eyes that she felt differently.

"Sure," I said, voicing Kat's thoughts because, for some reason, she couldn't. "Pizza sounds great."

CHAPTER FIVE

Pizza Palace was one of those restaurants tacked on to the side of the building as an afterthought. A place where people could still eat and not think they're in a food court or something. This particular restaurant stuck to the side of the Brookstone Mall. Memorabilia from Brookstone's past covered the walls. A ton of high school football and baseball photos. Images from the time the president visited the snowmobile factory outside of town. Taxidermy fish and deer and other animals thick with dust stared down at you while you devoured a deep-dish pepperoni.

Maybe eight or nine of us rode together over to the mall. Kat and I hitched a ride with Maisie and Arwen and Heidi, the sophomore in the lighting booth. We crammed in Maisie's tiny, cluttered car. It smelled like vanilla perfume.

Again, I just wanted to go home.

Kat, Arwen, and I were sandwiched in the back, with Kat in the middle. Her leg pressed against Arwen's, and I kept trying to not be obvious as I watched their reaction to one another. Still, nothing but the occasional friendly phrase or two.

A giant line of windows in Pizza Palace looked out on the mall. A long table ran alongside it. We sat down there, Kat and I facing out toward the other stores. Arwen sat across from Kat, sliding into her chair before someone else could take it. Zombified shoppers moved from one tacky clothing store to the next, all buying the same things, all looking the same way.

"I'm famished," William declared, plucking a menu from the middle of the table. The waitress, an older lady who looked like she didn't give two craps about working at a kitschy pizza joint, came over and took our order.

I sucked down my fountain drink, silent among the chatty friends.

"What did you guys think of the advanced chemistry test yesterday?" Quan asked. Even though he was a freshman, the kid was already in senior-level courses. He made me feel dumb.

A few others responded with "easy" and "a breeze." Which made me feel dumber, since I took the same test and pretty much filled in all the *C*s on my Scantron card.

"So, William," Maisie said, leaning forward in her seat. She had her legs tucked under her bottom and rested both elbows on the table. "Is your boyfriend coming to opening night?"

"He better," William answered. "And he better have a big old bouquet of flowers with him."

I knew that William was gay. He made no effort to hide it. "Loud, black, and proud," was his motto for pretty much everything—and that included being proud of his sexuality.

Our waitress dropped three baskets of breadsticks on our table. I took one and pulled it apart, its melted butter and crusted parm oozing onto my fingers.

"How about you, Arwen?" Maisie pressed. "Any chance this mysterious new lady friend of yours will come to the show?"

My ears perked up. I tried not to glance at Kat, but my eyes darted in her direction nonetheless. She seemed shell-shocked by the question. Thankfully, no one was staring at her but me.

Arwen laughed nervously. She didn't look at Kat. "We'll see," was all she said.

"She exists though, right?" William asked with a smile.

"Yeah, she exists," Arwen answered. And I could have sworn her eyes flitted over at Kat. They didn't linger, though. "She's actually pretty great."

"Aww," William said.

And that was it. No elaboration. No awkward follow-up questions. To these guys, Arwen having a girlfriend and William having a boyfriend was NBD. No big deal. But I guess Kat still needed some time.

The conversation shifted to a discussion on *Romeo & Juliet*. The DC-ers talked about how excited the cast was to get to dress rehearsals and when there would be costumes and makeup and everything would be finalized for the performances. The pizza came, rousing a cheer from the gang. They began to sing some song from a Broadway show I'd never seen, which made me slink down in my seat a bit.

Just then, a group of boys walked past Pizza Palace's enormous window. I spied Coen Marsh, Luke Best, and a few others. They looked over at the singing. Coen saw me sitting there in the middle of the chorus of voices and smiled. And it wasn't the smile that used to make my heart dance. The smile that used to make me wish I was a cheerleader, because why would a football player date me? A stupid thought, for sure, but one I couldn't lodge free from my head the whole time we dated.

No, this smile was more of an evil smirk. Like he'd caught me committing a crime.

Coen said something to his friends, and the whole group looked in the window, like Pizza Palace was a zoo and the DC-ers were its main attraction. They laughed, slapping each other on the shoulder.

I flipped them my patented one-finger salute. Both hands.

• • •

Afterward, Maisie drove us back to the school. Kat's busted-up car was one of the last in the lot. The ride had been her dad's old company car, bought for Kat after much begging and pleading. I chucked my bag in the backseat, which was cluttered with clothes and boots. Metal coffee thermoses on the floor rolled around and clanked against each other with each turn.

Kat handed me her phone. "Here," she said as she drove away from the school. "Find us something to listen to."

"How about show tunes?" I joked.

Kat laughed.

I searched for a playlist, found one full of punk bands with female lead singers, and started it.

"Perfect." Kat cranked up the volume, rolled her window down to let the chilly evening breeze fill the car and make her hair swirl, and drove.

We didn't say a word to one another, just sang songs together until Kat pulled into my driveway and thumbed the volume down on the stereo.

"So, uh . . . thanks again for coming," she said. "It'll be fun."

"Yeah," I said. "Who knew painting a fake castle with a bunch of awkward drama nerds could be a good time."

"Oh, come on," she said softly. "They're not *that* bad."

"No, I guess they're not." And the image of Kat reacting to Arwen's frank mention of her girlfriend popped into my head, followed by the image of Kat and Arwen in the car, pretending not to be close despite what I knew to be contrary.

I opened my mouth to say more. Now was the perfect time to tell Kat what I'd seen. I didn't care that she liked girls. I was *happy* that she found Arwen. Though I now wondered *how* they'd found each other. I wanted very much to ask Kat about it.

The soft, tinkling chime of Kat's phone stopped me. The phone, in its bloodred case, rested on the seat between us. It was closer to me than Kat, nearly touching my leg. Its screen glowed bright. Kat snatched the phone up before I could hand it to her. She looked at the message, then clicked it off. The blue glow illuminating her face winked out.

"Ugh," she said. "My mom's texting me." And just the way she said it, so off-handed and un-Kat-like, made me not believe her.

I knew it was Arwen.

She still doesn't want me to know.

I reached over the seat and grabbed my backpack. "See ya tomorrow," I said as I opened the door.

"Yeah," Kat said, phone still clutched in her hand. "See ya."

Mom and Dad were in their usual spots in the downstairs family room. The two of them lounged on the couch, watching some silly reality dating show. The pained look on my dad's face said it all: tonight's viewing pleasure was Mom's choice. Ike and Beck were already in bed.

"So what were you and Kat up to tonight?" my dad asked. His voice pleaded with me, like he desperately wanted someone to talk to him about something other than what he'd been subjected to.

"Drama club," I answered. "Then pizza at the Palace."

Dad laughed.

I didn't crack a smile.

"Wait," he said, sitting up, "Seriously?"

"Yeah, seriously," I said. "Kat and I volunteered to help paint some sets. NBD."

"That's wonderful," Mom said.

"Yeah, well, don't get used to it." I smiled, then retreated to my room to relax. There was homework in my bag—some Civics worksheets from Mrs. Voss—but I wasn't planning on doing them.

After scrolling through my phone, more bored than ever, I found myself walking down the hall to my dad's office. It was dark and musty and cluttered with shelves of books. Both of my parents were avid readers, and their collection practically spilled out into the hall. I clicked on the light and rummaged around until I found a thick, dusty hardcover made of dark blue leather.

The Annotated Plays of William Shakespeare.

I took the hefty book back to my room, laid down on my bed, and cracked it open. *Romeo & Juliet* was somewhere in the middle. The book's tiny font and numerous footnotes made it more than intimidating to read.

But I tried anyway.

I was slogging through Act One when my phone buzzed on the nightstand.

Bzzzt-bzzzt. Bzzzt-bzzzt.

I rolled over and checked.

It was from Coen.

HAVE FUN HANGING W UR NEW FRIENDS?

"Great," I muttered. I tossed the phone back down. I wasn't going to give him the satisfaction of responding.

And then another text came in.

U SWITCHING TEAMS? INTO GIRLS NOW?

This one made my cheeks burn red and my hands shake. Coen was an idiot, and I regretted ever agreeing to go on a date with him, let alone calling him my boyfriend for two months.

I picked up my phone. Set it down. Picked it up again. Typed.

LEAVE ME ALONE, JERK.

I flung my phone toward my open closet door where my laundry basket sat overflowing like a cotton-spewing volcano. The phone struck with a quiet *thunk*, then slid down between the clothes. I wasn't going to poke the stupid bear.

After, I couldn't quite seem to concentrate on Bill Shakespeare. It was giving me a headache. So I slammed the book closed, changed into some pajamas, and instead of completing my nightly routine of checking my phone to see if Kat had any final thoughts on the day, I rolled into bed.

I already knew the only texts I'd see would be the ones from Coen.

CHAPTER SIX

My dad had a two-honk rule. If Ike, Beck, or I was running late for school and Dad was in the car, ready to leave for work, he'd honk. If we didn't make it out before honk number two, we'd have to take the bus. Dad's commute was already forty-five minutes in gridlock. If we ran late, so did he.

So the next morning, when I heard the second honk, I panicked. I hated the bus, despised being trapped inside a giant metal deathtrap, surrounded by kids I didn't like. I ran through the kitchen, wet hair and all, grabbed my backpack off the hook by the door, and barged out into the garage, leaving the brown bag lunch my mom so lovingly made before she left for her own early-morning commute sitting on the counter.

And that's why, when the lunch bell rang that afternoon, I was forced to eat the least vile cafeteria food I could find. I opted for a salad drowning in sunflower seeds and French dressing and a ham and Swiss sandwich wrapped in cellophane.

On days when I didn't bring lunch, Kat and I would typically duck out and drive down to the bagel shop. Lots of older kids did. But Kat had a doctor's appointment that day and wasn't going to be back until the afternoon.

I searched the crowded cafeteria for a spot to sit. There was an empty table near the back, hidden from view by a brick pillar.

Perfect.

As I wove through the rows of tables, though, I spied Arwen sitting by herself at the end of a table. She had her head down, hair falling in front of her face, writing in a notebook. She didn't see me. I could waltz right past her and she wouldn't notice.

I stopped. Fought with myself. Sighed.

"What are you doing?" I asked myself as I changed course and abandoned the empty table and all its solitary glory.

I dropped my tray on the table across from Arwen and sat. She jolted up, sweeping her hair away from her face with one hand while closing the notebook with the other. Its red cover was filled with doodles, arrows and cubes and stuff.

"Oh," she said when she saw who'd broken her concentration. "Hi, Dessa."

"Hey." I began to unwrap my sandwich, knowing already that I wasn't going to eat much of it. "Where's the rest of the DC-ers?"

"Late lunch bell," she said. Then, after a long pause, "Um . . . where's Kat?"

"Doctor."

"Oh."

I felt completely out of place sitting with Arwen. We had nothing in common. Well, one thing, and I suppose that was why I was there. I wanted to find out what made this girl so special. What made her tick. What attracted a girl like Kat to her.

I nodded at the closed notebook. "Whatcha writing?"

Arwen chewed on her bottom lip, like she was trying to decide whether or not to trust me. "It's . . . a short story for English class," she said. I still couldn't tell if it was the truth or not. She had her guard up, and I couldn't blame her. This was the most we'd ever spoken.

"Cool." I broke off a piece of cold and slightly soggy bread and popped it into my mouth. I immediately regretted it. "You write a lot?"

Arwen shrugged. "Yeah, I guess."

I felt like I was in one of those interrogation scenes on a cop show, like I was trying to pry valuable information out of a suspect. I decided to go right to the heart of the matter.

"So during the chatter at the Palace, I heard you have a girlfriend," I said. "That's cool."

That did it. Arwen sat back in her chair. Crossed her arms at her chest. Protective. "Yeah," she said, hesitant.

"Look, I'm not judging," I said, throwing my hands up, palms out. "Nobody has the right to judge anyone else. Not unless they've walked a mile . . . or whatever." Arwen looked around, probably wishing the second lunch bell would ring and her real friends would show up and save her. "How'd you meet?" I asked.

She bit her bottom lip again. If I was playing poker against her, I'd know her tell right away. "Oh . . . " she started, "Mrs. Updahl grouped us together for a creative writing assignment. We met one day after school, and the other two kids flaked on us."

I remembered this part of Updahl's class. I was in a different period, so I had been grouped with Luke Best, Ramona, and Erika Wenk, a violin-playing orchestra girl. It had happened near the start of the school year, almost two months ago.

Is that how long Kat's been keeping this from me? I wondered, that stab of hurt finding my heart again.

Arwen was still talking. ". . . and then we just got to talking and . . . well . . ."

"So she goes to Brookstone?" Like I didn't know the answer.

Arwen's cheeks flushed red, as though she'd revealed too much already. "Yeah. But, like . . . don't tell anyone, okay? Not yet. She's not out or anything."

I pressed my index finger and thumb together, then mimed zipping my lips closed. "And I'm tossing out the key," I said.

And then the table shifted. It felt like an earthquake jolted us back. My tray skidded off the table, into my lap. Wilted lettuce, sunflower seeds, and the gamma-radiated bright orange of

French dressing coated my jeans.

A group of boys had been walking past, Coen and Luke Best and the same jerks we'd seen at the mall the night before. Coen had pushed Luke into our table. He bent over laughing, his elbows on the tabletop.

"Oh," Luke said sarcastically. "So sorry, ladies."

"Did we interrupt your date?" Coen asked. He helped Luke back up. As he did, his meaty hand pressed down on Arwen's red notebook. She opened her mouth to say something, then didn't. I picked the tray from my lap. I wanted nothing more than to shove it back into his chest, smear whatever food was left on it into his ugly shirt.

Coen swiped his hand across the table, sending Arwen's notebook skittering onto the linoleum floor. It disappeared under another table.

"Oops," he said. I saw the look in Arwen's eyes as she stood up, swallowing back tears.

Say something, I urged her. *Do something.*
Anything.

Instead, she walked over past Coen and his cohorts, over to the table. "Excuse me," I heard her say meekly as she crouched down on hands and knees to retrieve her notebook.

"You're a real class act," I said to Coen as he, Luke, and the others started to walk away.

"Hey, McKenzie," Coen said, ignoring me, "Let me know if you need any kissing tips. I know *just* what Kingston likes." He smacked his lips together as the others laughed again.

I walked over, found some stray napkins on a table, and wiped the salad bits off my jeans. I balled them up and threw them in the direction of Coen, but he was well out of reach by then.

"You okay?" I asked Arwen, even though all I could see of her was her backside and legs as she crawled under the table.

"Fine," she answered.

A few people sat at the other end of the

table, and they were doing nothing to help. In fact, they acted like Arwen was invisible.

"Come on," I said, nudging a vapid senior girl named Harper. "Out of her way. Can't you see there's someone physically crawling around on the floor?"

Harper said nothing, but her face scrunched up in annoyance before she scooted aside.

Arwen backed out from under the table. She had the notebook, but I could see smudges of ink on the cover now. She wiped it off with one sleeve of her sweater and stood.

A tone sounded in the cafeteria, indicating that the late lunch folks would soon be joining us. That meant reinforcements: Arwen's real friends.

I looked her up and down and once more asked, "Are you all right?"

She looked like she could cry, like the dam could burst at any moment. "I said I'm fine," she repeated. "It's not like this is the first time Coen Marsh has targeted me."

"Well that's just stupid," I said. "You gotta stand up for yourself, Arwen. I mean, more often than not. It's not like anyone else is going to do it."

"Yeah," she said, walking back over and sitting down. I shoved aside the goop-filled chair I'd been sitting in and grabbed a new one, wondering why I hadn't heeded my own advice.

CHAPTER SEVEN

The remainder of the day was uneventful. I wish I could say the rest of the week went the same way.

It didn't.

On Wednesday, Quan came into the auditorium looking distraught. In his hand was a stack of pink flyers. "Somebody's been tearing our signs off the walls," he said. He held up the flyers and shook them. "These are just the ones I picked up off the floor. I found a whole bunch of them in the boys' bathroom next to the gym. They were in the . . . well . . ."

He didn't have to finish his sentence. And

even though we didn't know the culprit, it was pretty obvious to me who'd done it.

Then, as William walked into the auditorium on Friday, I could tell something was wrong. He wasn't his usual, jovial self. But then Maisie gasped when she hugged him, and said, "Oh, my God. William, what happened?"

The DC-ers all ditched what they were doing and crowded around William and Maisie near the orchestra pit.

Under William's left eye was a purplish bruise.

"Gym class Neanderthals," William said off-handedly. "The risks of playing handball."

"Someone hit you?" Quan asked.

"Our good friend Coen Marsh, actually. We were both going for the ball, and his elbow 'accidentally' found its way into my eye. Yay, me!"

I shook my head in disgust.

"Now," William said, "Let's get to work, shall we?"

And so we did.

When Kat and I had finished painting the castle, we went to work building a set for the tomb where the two lovebirds croak. (Spoiler alert.) That was actually a bunch of fun, making the wood look like stone, building a sarcophagus for them, and draping the set in fake cobwebs.

The following week left just a few days until opening night. At practice, the actors all came on set in costume and makeup. Mr. Baker had them run through the entire show from start to finish. Kat and I stood backstage. "Cool," I said. "If they don't need us, we can probably jet."

Kat shook her head. "Can we stay?" she asked. "Mr. Baker said anyone who wants to can sit in the auditorium. I want to watch the show."

"Okay," I said, surprised at how easy it was to convince me. "We can stay."

But as Mr. Baker prepped some freshmen

for the fight scene that opened the play, Arwen found me and Kat sitting in the second row and jumped down off the stage to join us. "Hey, guys," she whispered.

Kat sat up in her seat a bit, eager to answer. "Yeah?"

"We're gonna need a few hands moving sets around. Do you want to help?"

"Sure," I said, not looking at Kat, knowing what she'd say anyway.

So we stayed and watched but did it from backstage. I never realized what went on behind the scenes. So much work. It was like a dance. Actors moved back and forth across the darkened backstage area, lit by small blue lights. Arwen was in her element. She called lighting cues on the microphone, positioned actors, and directed us where to be for each set change.

It was then that I saw a glimmer of her confidence, saw why Kat would be attracted to her. She looked so very different than the meek girl I saw in the cafeteria.

The morning before the show opened, Mr. Baker held his traditional screening for the rest of the school. Much like *Fiddler* last year, he wanted to show a fast-paced scene filled with action. So he chose the first fight between the Capulets and the Montagues.

Since the preview screening didn't include a set change, Kat and I weren't needed backstage. So we sat in the crowd of tired kids, down near the front but a bit off stage right. I noticed Coen Marsh and Luke Best a few rows behind us.

After a brief introduction by Mr. Baker, the house lights dimmed. "Ooooh, setting the mood," I heard Coen say. I rolled my eyes.

A.J. Sparks and Keaton Best—Luke's younger brother and exact opposite—strolled on stage. From the other side came a couple of other awkward freshmen, Christian North and Ben Wallenstein. I heard snickers travel through the crowd. As the actors argued with one another, the crowd grew a bit restless. But then swords were drawn and a fight began. Metal clashed with metal. One boy hoisted his arm on another's hip and dropped him solidly to the stage.

From behind me, Coen said, "Look at them slapping each other up there. Embarrassing."

I clutched my armrests, dug my fingers in, wanted to turn around and say something so the entire auditorium could hear.

Because I was getting really tired of Coen Marsh.

* * *

Opening night arrived on the first bitterly cold day of the fall. A Thursday. *Romeo & Juliet* would run all weekend, five shows total including a matinee on Sunday, closing with a Monday night performance. I stopped home after school, planning on being back an hour before curtain. Stagehands typically wore a black shirt and black pants so they would blend in. I didn't have a problem finding that in my closet. And it was then I realized something.

I was actually nervous about opening night.

Kat waited in the car while I changed. Before dashing out the door, I left a note for my parents. *4 tickets at will-call*, I scribbled. Mom and Dad were very excited about coming. Ike and Beck? Probably not so much.

The dressing rooms adjacent to the auditorium were abuzz with activity. The entire cast had crowded in there, singing along to a playlist of musical theater tunes piping out of a pair of small speakers. The performers were in various stages of dress. Some of the younger, more eager freshmen and sophomores were already costumed up. Others wore thick makeup but hadn't put on their outfits yet.

"*Hello, little girl!*" William sang as he saw us. He grabbed me by the waist and danced with me. "*What's your rush? You're missing all the flowers . . .* " He smelled like thick pancake foundation, and I could see it was covering his black eye pretty well. His leather costume issued a mixture of sweat and must.

I laughed, a genuine sound of glee. He spun me around until I was dizzy, then dipped me so low my hair brushed the floor.

"Fifteen minutes, everyone!" Arwen shouted as she bustled through the dressing room area. Her ever-present binder was hooked in one arm. When she saw Kat, she tucked her hair behind one ear and quietly said, "Hey, Kat."

"Hi," Kat responded with a smile. She seemed miles more comfortable around Arwen now than she had when we first wielded paintbrushes oh so long ago. "Good luck tonight."

"Thanks."

Kat and I hung out backstage with the other stagehands, plotting out how we were going to move the sets. From behind the thick velour curtain, I could hear feet shuffling and the quiet sounds of conversation as the auditorium began to fill with people. I wondered if my parents and brothers were among them yet. I hoped they'd get a good seat.

I don't even know who I am anymore.

Finally, Mr. Baker gathered us all in the small area between the dressing rooms and the stage. "Form a circle," he said. We did. "All of your hard work has led us to this moment. Be proud of what you've accomplished. Project your pride to the farthest corners of the auditorium. Let the audience bathe in it. All together now." He paused. "Energy . . . pace . . . enthusiasm."

And the rest of the cast and crew joined in. "*Energy . . . pace . . . enthusiasm!*" they chanted. Quan leaped up and down, and others joined in. The junior playing Tybalt, Max Goodman, raised both hands in the air. "*Energy . . . pace . . . enthusiasm!*"

Beside me, Kat began to jump and shout along. I did too.

We ended our pre-show circle with a rousing cheer and an enormous group hug.

A group hug.

I was part of a group hug.

My life had become exceptionally bizarre.

"All right," I said to Riannon, who had her arms wrapped around me, squeezing like a boa constrictor. "That's enough."

Finally, the actors took their places as we stood backstage. Arwen whispered to Heidi up in the lighting booth, "House lights down." Then, as a hush fell over the crowd, "Stage lights up." An unearthly glow spilled from beneath the curtain.

Arwen turned to the nervous freshmen whose argument started the show and said, "Keaton. A.J. Break a leg." Then she pointed to Quan, who had both hands on a thick rope. He jumped up and pulled it down. The velour curtain began to open, and a dazzling light turned the world upside down.

It was—and forgive me for using a word I

never in a million years thought I would ever use—*magical.* For the next two and half hours, William, Maisie, and the entire drama club owned the stage. The audience laughed and gasped and applauded at every chance. And when the lights went down between scenes, Kat and I would move sets in darkness. Once, I could have sworn I heard my mom whisper, "There she is!"

When the final act concluded, when the star-crossed lovers lay dead across one another in the tomb while their families mourned and the curtain closed around them, the crowd rose to its feet. Their applause was intoxicating.

The actors lined up on stage and bowed in groups of two or four. When William and Maisie took their turn, the shouts and catcalls rose. A male voice shouted, "I love you, William!" which drew nervous laughs from those who didn't know the voice belonged to William's boyfriend and genuine laughs from those who did. I kinda wanted to walk out there myself, haul Kat and Arwen and Quan with me, and take our own moment to bask in the spotlight.

Then I thought better, remembered how much I preferred the shadows, and watched as the cast came together and took one last bow.

CHAPTER EIGHT

"Oh my God, that was so *amazing*!" William shouted at the top of his lungs. He stuck his head out the passenger side window of Kat's car like a dog on a joyride. "Thank you, Brookstone!" he bellowed, laughing deeply.

Kat drove through the middle of town, past the mall and out toward County Road 73. I sat in the backseat alongside Arwen and William's boyfriend, Ephram. Quan's car honked twice behind us. William blew them a kiss.

Maisie's family lived outside of town, and even though it was a school night, the whole cast and crew was heading out there for the club's traditional opening night cast party. When I'd mentioned it to my parents post-show, my mom had immediately said, "Go. Have fun."

Maisie led the caravan. Her taillights were two cars ahead of us.

County Road 73 met up with Central at the edge of town, where two-story motels and the mall and the giant box stores turned to cornfields and trees whose leaves burned red and orange and yellow. Our headlights cut through the pitch black as we wove down the two-lane highway.

Then, ahead of us, Maisie's taillights went dark.

"Whoa! What's going on?" I asked.

"Is she okay?" Kat added. She must have lifted her foot off the gas pedal, because I felt the car slowly lose speed.

William cackled. "It's a tradition!" he said. "Kill the house lights!" He leaned over, reached for Kat's steering wheel, and found the switch for the headlights. He twisted it, leaving us driving forty miles an hour in the dead of night down a winding road with no lights.

Kat and I screamed. "You're insane!" I shouted. I spun in my seat, saw a line of cars behind us. One by one, they all did the same. "You're all insane!"

"We all go a little mad sometimes," William said, howling with laughter.

When my eyes adjusted, I could still see the road. Could still see Maisie in front of us, driving slower.

I was actually mad at myself for being scared. So I rolled down my window and, like William, stuck my head out to holler at the cloudless sky. Behind us, one car started honking. Then another. Then a third. Finally Kat joined the chorus.

We passed through a heavily-wooded area that I was kind of familiar with, mostly because there was a trestle bridge out on 73 that I'd partied at when I was dating Coen. Then the trees disappeared, replaced by a high wooden fence and acres of open land.

Maisie's headlights flared back to life. Kat quickly did the same with hers.

"Wait. Maisie's family owns Brookstone Stables?" I asked.

"Yep," William said. "You didn't know that?"

"Do I seem like someone who pays attention to those kinds of things?"

"Touché," he answered.

We turned into the driveway under a wooden sign with *BISHOP STABLES* carved into it, moving down a long gravel road.

Maisie's parents were home, but they actually went to bed shortly after we arrived. Their house had a spacious downstairs area decked out in all things rustic. Huge horse paintings in ornate frames filled the walls. A wooden bookcase sat against one wall, made of the same weathered planks used on the fence surrounding the property. Horseshoe bookends sat on its shelves, and woven throw blankets were draped on leather furniture.

There was a billiards table in the back of the family room, an expensive-looking one with brown felt instead of green. A.J., Keaton, and a few other freshmen went straight for it, like they were being sucked into a dude vortex. A giant television was mounted on the wall above a stone fireplace. Soon it was playing old British comedy by a group called Monty Python. I didn't know who they were, but apparently they were *hilarious*. Pretty much everyone there except me and Kat knew every line, every joke.

"I gotta use the bathroom," Kat said quietly, looking around. "Maisie?"

Maisie said, "Down the hall, second door on the left. It's super-barfy. My mom decorated it after she and Dad came back from Belize, so it's all conch shells and blue paint and framed photos of islands." She added, "There's even a wooden parrot over the sink."

I laughed as Kat disappeared down the hall, then helped Maisie grab some sodas and snacks from a bar and pantry. Neon beer signs hung all around, mirrors with Clydesdale horses on them. It took me a moment to notice that Arwen had vanished too.

I sat on the arm of the couch where Quan, Heidi, and Max sat together, singing along with the television to some song about lumberjacks. William and Ephram fell into a plush easy chair together, twining their legs and speaking to each other in low tones.

Finally, I saw Arwen and Kat return, one before the other, from wherever they'd really escaped to. Just another one of those subtle, sneaky moves I'd grown used to seeing. Kat wedged her way onto the couch beside me. Arwen stood near the bar, sipping from a bottle of water.

The buzz from that night's performance was still going strong. Everyone spoke in loud voices, like they were still projecting to the last row. I could feel the buzz coursing through my veins too.

"Ugh," Ephram said, his hands cupping William's face. "I can't believe what that monster did to your beautiful face."

"Oh, stop," William said. "I'm fine."

"I bet he wouldn't have done it if he'd known you had a second-level black belt."

"Wait. You know kung fu?" I asked with a smile.

William shook his head. "Tae kwon do. And it's not like I'm an action star or anything."

"Please," Ephram said. "I've seen the way those legs move. Your kicks are fierce." He turned to me. "That's how we met, you know," he said. "Breaking boards and looking good doing it. Our sensei paired us together."

"Hey," I said, placing an arm on Kat's shoulder, "That's kind of like how you and Arwen met. Paired together on . . ."

"What?" Kat's voice was barely a whisper.

The moment the words fled my lips, I wanted to snatch them back out of the air. I don't know why I said it. Maybe it was the lingering adrenaline from being on stage or the camaraderie between friends, but the comment slipped out way too easily.

"Oh . . . um . . . " I didn't know how to backtrack, but it didn't matter. Kat could see it in my eyes.

"You know." I could almost feel the air shatter around Kat as she realized what I'd said.

"Know what?" Quan asked, leaping unknowingly into our very serious moment.

Kat brushed my hand from her shoulder and quickly stood. "I've gotta . . . I've gotta go," she said. She used the sleeve of her black sweatshirt to wipe her eyes. Then she rushed to the stairs.

"Kat!" I called after her. "Wait!"

I hurried up the stairs, heard the whisk and slam of the heavy front door closing. I could feel the DC-ers' eyes on me as I followed.

A few kids whispered questions in Arwen's direction.

And then I was outside, rushing down the gravel driveway in the cold. "Kit-Kat," I said, seeing her almost at her car.

She didn't stop. I saw her shoulders shudder and realized that she was crying.

I ran as fast as I could. "Kat," I said. "I'm so sorry."

"Go away, Dessa!" She spun around to face me, anger in her eyes, cheeks flushed red and covered in tears. "Leave me alone!"

"I didn't mean to say anything," I explained. "I was waiting until you—"

"Waiting? So how long have you known?"

"I . . . I . . . "

"How long!?"

My shoulders sagged. "Since the day we met at the rocks. I saw you and Arwen in the auditorium."

"You were spying on us?" She fumbled in her pocket for her car keys. They jingled nervously in her shaking hands.

"No," I said. "Look, I'm happy for you. I am. Yeah, I'm still trying to figure out the best way to show my support, and I'm wondering why you didn't tell me, but I don't care anymore, Kit-Kat."

"Stop calling me that," she said. She looked past me, toward the house. I turned and saw a few of the DC-ers standing in the window, peering through blinds.

"Great," Kat said. "Now everyone knows."

"Who cares?" I asked.

"I do! I'm not ready to be looked at this way. To be called names and treated differently by my family . . . " she trailed off. Fresh tears welled in her eyes. I went in to hug her, and she shoved me back.

"Find somebody else to drive you home," she said, opening the driver's side door with a creak. "I don't want to talk to you right now."

"Come on, Kat," I tried once more, knowing full-well it wasn't going to work.

"Goodbye, Dessa." And with a slam, Kat cranked her car's engine to life, whipped around in a U-turn, and drove off.

* * *

Max Goodman gave me a ride home. He was tall and his car was tiny, so when he sat behind the wheel, it was almost comical. He wore a plain white T-shirt emblazoned with the logo for the school's marching band. A large case holding either a tuba or a dead body filled the entire backseat.

He was nervous the whole way, fidgeting with the radio and apologizing for the lack of good music. I wondered briefly if he thought we were on a date, or that he was going to score when we pulled into my driveway. Maybe he just wasn't used to having a girl riding beside him.

Every ounce of joy I'd experienced that night was washed out of me. I clutched my phone tight, hoping for Kat to call, but she didn't.

When Max pulled into my driveway, I quickly opened the door. "Thanks for the lift," I muttered.

"See you tomorrow at school!" He tried to sound cheerful, but it wasn't having any effect on me.

I was heartbroken.

CHAPTER NINE

I barely slept. I kept twisting and turning in bed. My sheets felt thick, pressing down on my legs and chest. I remember kicking them off until they slid onto the floor at some point. I checked my phone several times, hoping to see a text from Kat.

Nothing.

I started to write one to her, then thought better of it.

Also, I'll admit, I cried.

When the sun cracked through the slats of my window blinds, I'd maybe gotten an hour of sleep. I could practically feel the bags under my burning eyes.

"I see someone enjoyed celebrating the show's success last night," Dad said, sipping from a coffee mug as I walked like a zombie into the kitchen.

"Yeah," was all I could muster. I didn't want to get into it.

Ike and Beck rushed past me on the way out the door, arguing about Legos and ninjas and the stupid stuff that little dudes argue about. Kat and I have had plenty of silly disagreements over the years. They blew over. They always did.

Will this blow over too?

This was serious. Kat had never yelled at me the way she did the night before. I'd done something pretty awful, even if I hadn't meant to.

When I walked into school, I didn't even think about hitting my locker to drop off my bag. Instead, I beelined it toward Kat's. I was determined to camp out there until she showed up.

No camping was necessary, though. As I rounded the corner, I spied Kat standing beside her open locker. Arwen was there too, along with William and Maisie and a handful of other students. Some random classmates passed by. Some loitered at their lockers. And a tall, thickly-built jerk was facing Kat.

"Ugh . . . Coen," I muttered, coming to a stop.

Coen Marsh was in full-harassment mode already, and it wasn't even eight a.m.

"Is it true?" he asked loudly. "Are you a lesbian, Kat?"

"How . . . how did you . . . " Kat stammered.

"Luke's bro told him last night, and he dropped me a text. Said you and Dessa got into it after you came out." He stepped closer to her. "Is it true?"

"Well . . . "

"Oh, my God!" he shouted for the whole crowd to hear. "Kat Beckford is totally a lesbo!"

Kids snickered. Whispered to one another.

It felt as though one of the auditorium spotlights was shining right on Kat. I walked fast down the hall, wondering why there wasn't a teacher around.

"Come on, Kat," Arwen said as she threaded her fingers into Kat's. Kat quickly shook her hand free.

"Man, don't you two look hot together." Coen stepped between them. "Where are you going? I need to know all of the steamy details."

"Leave them alone." William came in from the right, his voice loud to match Coen's level.

Coen placed a meaty hand on William's chest and shoved him away. "Back off, queer." William slammed into the row of lockers and fell to the floor. A tiny gasp of pain escaped his lips.

That was it.

I'd had enough.

"Hey!" I shouted. The crowd turned in my

direction, Coen included. I strode forward, my legs full of power and anger and my hands squeezing into fists at my side.

Coen gave me a smug look when he saw who'd interrupted his little game. He opened his mouth to say something, but before he could, I lashed out with both fists, right at his chest. Coen stumbled backward.

"How do *you* like it?" I asked through gritted teeth.

"*Fight! Fight! Fight!*" Around us, the haphazard group of kids had morphed into a chanting mob. A few of Coen's pals looked ready to join in against the DC-ers, if necessary. We were like the Capulets and Montagues, except the combat wasn't staged.

Coen lurched toward me. I didn't know what his intention was, but I wasn't going to find out.

I swung my right fist and felt the jolt as it connected to Coen's nose.

He coughed, violent and sharp, and

brought his hands to his face. "Ib's brogan," he said in a garbled voice. A stream of blood leaked between his fingers as his hands cupped his face. "You broge my nobe!"

"Oh, my God, Dessa," Kat said from behind me. "What did you do?"

I didn't know I was going to punch him. But I sure as hell didn't feel sorry about it. Coen deserved that lovely little present.

"What's going on here?" The crowd scattered like cockroaches under a light. Mr. Leonard, a freshman Spanish teacher, stood there. His red face had scrunched up in a look that was equal parts anger and confusion. Especially when he saw my fist and Coen's nose.

I looked around, trying to find Kat in the crowd. William was there. Maisie was helping him to his feet. The purple bruise beneath his eye seemed to stand out even more than it had the night before.

But there was no sign of Kat. She was gone.

My shoulders sagged. My fists unwound. My adrenaline evaporated.

It was too late, though.

* * *

The chair in Principal Yang's office was old and lumpy, its wooden arms smoothed from years of worried students clutching them like I was doing now.

Principal Yang sat across the desk from me, staring me down like she thought silence was going to break me. A manila folder containing my school record lay open in front of her. The rest of her desk was neat, tidy, all perfect angles and not a paper clip out of place.

My mom burst through the door not five minutes later. She was a whirlwind, hair and coat and scarf blowing back. She did nothing but apologize, not wanting to hear my side of the story. I watched as she listened to Yang, nodding and saying things like, "We're so sorry" and "She *knows* better" and "There's no reason to resort to violence."

Finally, when Mom was done pleading and butt-kissing, Principal Yang said, "Mrs. Kingston. Dessa. As you well know, Brookstone has a zero-tolerance policy when it comes to violence. I've decided that, in this case, Dessa's penalty will be an immediate ten-day suspension."

"Yeah, well what's your *policy* on bullying?" I countered, leaning forward in my seat. My blood was on fire, and I wasn't going to leave without a fight. "Because Coen Marsh has been harassing my friends for weeks now." I didn't realize I was going to use the word *friends* until it was out of my mouth.

"Miss Kingston, I'm sorry if you or any of your friends have been the target of bullying. Obviously, had we known—"

"It was so obvious!" I slammed a fist on Principal Yang's desk.

"Miss Kingston," she said, beginning to lose her cool. "I suggest you calm down."

"Dessa," Mom added, placing a hand on my shoulder.

I ignored them. "And today? Today was just the icing on the cake. Coen Marsh, this bigoted, ignorant creep, instigated the *entire thing*! Why isn't *he* in here instead of me?"

"Because he's currently in the hospital emergency room," Principal Yang nearly shouted, standing to face me, "where doctors are resetting the broken nose *you* gave him."

The office grew thick with silence.

"Now, if you're finished," Principal Yang continued, her eyes boring holes into me, "I believe I need to assess a few things over the weekend, including whether or not Brookstone High is still a good fit for you, Miss Kingston."

"What?" Her words felt like a splash of cold water on my face.

"Do you mean . . . *expulsion*?" Mom let out a long, ragged breath. She was fighting back tears. "You can't just . . ."

"I'm sorry, Mrs. Kingston," Principal Yang said. "I'll be in touch very soon."

The anger I felt when Coen shoved William, when he laughed at Kat and Arwen, had been replaced by fear and confusion. I backed away from Principal Yang's desk, nearly knocking my chair over backward. "So unfair," I hissed.

Then I was out the door, my apologetic mom at my heels, the hall outside the office empty. I trudged back to the parking lot and to my mom's waiting car and a long, quiet ride home.

CHAPTER TEN

Dad was expecting us when we walked in the door. He sat at the dining room table, suit coat draped over the chair next to him, tie loosened. He looked like a man waiting for a meal that was never going to come. It would have been comical if not for the disappointment on his face. And with Ike and Beck at school, the house was eerily silent.

I dropped my backpack on the table, sat down, and tucked my legs underneath me. Dad leaned forward, placing his hands atop one another on the table. "Explain yourself," he said.

So I did. I told them everything. Well, not

everything. I left out the most important part, actually. The part about Kat's secret. But I told them about joining the DC-ers, about painting sets, and about Coen Marsh targeting us. When I explained how William got his black eye, Mom finally sat beside me. And when I reached the end, the punch and the broken nose, I could see a hint of sympathy in their eyes.

Dad cleared his throat. "Dessa," he said. "Your mother and I"—he looked to her for agreement, and she nodded—"understand your need to defend your friends. But hitting a kid? Breaking his nose? We'll be lucky if his family doesn't press charges."

"Awesome," I said. "I've once again found a way to disappoint you, even though I was doing the right thing."

"Dessa, we're not disappointed," Mom said.

"So . . . can I be excused?" I asked.

"Yes." Dad leaned back in his chair.

I gathered my things and trudged to my bedroom.

∎ ∎ ∎

Still no word from Kat.

I kept my phone in front of me on the bed, kept staring at it, willing it to buzz. But you know what they saw about a watched cell phone never boiling. Or something like that.

As mid-afternoon came and went, I wondered what version of the story was being passed around Brookstone High. The truth? Or some warped game of telephone that made Coen Marsh the victim and me the bully? This was more likely the case, because who was more likely to be telling the truth: a popular meathead or his angry ex-girlfriend?

I thought about the DC-ers and how they were all making their way to the dressing rooms for the Friday night performance. Were they talking about this morning's incident? Was Kat with them? Or was she too embarrassed to show up anymore?

So in the dark. I'd never felt so helpless in my life.

But I could change that.

If I wanted to stand in the spotlight and have my voice heard, there were ways to do it.

And so I plucked my quiet phone off the bedspread. Sure, I wasn't allowed at school. But that didn't mean I couldn't state my case somehow. I thumbed through my apps, switched my camera to video, and pressed the circular, red record button.

"Hey, it's Dessa Kingston," I started, my face on the screen looking back at me. "You've probably heard a lot of rumors about me. About my sexuality. About my friends. And, well, probably about my right hook. I did what I did because I care about my friends. Because everyone should be able to live and love equally, without being judged. Because bullying should never be tolerated. And because everyone should have *someone* who stands up for them.

"This is my story . . . "

* * *

Bzzzt-bzzzt. Bzzzt-bzzzt.

My phone was vibrating off the hook, and I'd only uploaded the video an hour ago.

The first message came from William: *MY DEAR, SWEET DESSA, WHOSE FIST HATH SLAIN THE SAVAGE BEAST, THANK U.*

Another, from Maisie: *WE MISS U. TONIGHT'S PERFORMANCE IS 4 U.*

And right before the house lights were set to go down and Quan was to pull back the curtains, a simple message from Arwen: *THANX.*

But nothing from Kat.

Kids I'd never met before were leaving comments of their own on my video. Some from Brookstone. Kids I saw in the lunchroom or sat next to in class. Others from states away. I'd touched a nerve, and it was going viral.

And then, finally, as midnight crept in and my eyelids were getting heavy, the phone buzzed one last time. I didn't even need to check to see who it was, but I did anyway.

I'M OUTSIDE. CAN U SNEAK OUT?

I wrote back right away. *OF COURSE.*

Mom and Dad hit the sack every night after the local weather lady gave them the forecast. So they had already departed for dream land. Ike and Beck were tucked away too, all snuggled in their bunk beds, their bedroom floor a minefield of Legos and action figures. I made my way down the hall to the darkened dining room, not caring to flick on any lights. I cracked open the sliding patio door that led to our backyard. A blast of cold air hit me right away, and I slid my hands into my hoodie pocket.

"Kit-Kat?" I hissed.

"Over here." I saw her in the moonlight. She was sitting in one of the wooden Adirondack chairs Mom always had out by the garden, near the swing set. She wore a heavy coat. A floppy stocking cap, the kind with the giant puff ball on top, was perched on her head.

I slid into the chair beside her. "Brrr," I said.

"I think it was snowing a bit earlier," Kat said. "Tiny flakes."

"Oh, God. I hope not. I'm so not ready for snow." Well, actually, I was never ready. I hated the cold, same as Kat.

"Arwen's family are all big skiers and snowboarders," Kat said, pulling down her stocking cap. "She told me she would teach me how to ski this winter."

"Fun."

"I . . . I'm not ready to tell my parents yet, Dessa. Soon, I hope."

"Okay," I said. "I'll be here for you when you do."

"I know."

And then we sat in silence. It was like the world was shifting on its axis, back to its rightful place again. Sitting there in the dark, staring up at the stars, I brought my knees to my chest and wrapped my arms around them.

I could see my breath in front of me. But I wasn't uncomfortable. Not in the least. I never was with Kat. No matter the situation, no matter if we were fighting over stupid things or something as life-changing as this, we could always sit in each other's company and just . . . be.

Regardless of who we were becoming.

* * *

Monday morning.

I was sitting at the kitchen island, a soggy bowl of cereal in front of me, watching some boring news show on the small television hanging under one of the cabinets. Mom rushed around, getting ready to head out the door. Dad hummed as he made Ike and Beck their lunches.

"Let's go, troops!" he shouted to my brothers, who were fighting for a few more minutes of playtime before getting their shoes on.

"All right," they grumbled in unison.

And that was when Mom's phone began to ring.

Everything in our house came to a screeching stop. Dad stood with his peanut-butter-covered knife held high. Mom had one arm in her coat, the other free. From my spot at the island, I could see that the caller ID read: *BROOKSTONE HIGH.*

"You . . . uh . . . you gonna get that?" I asked.

Mom, coat draped over one shoulder, answered. "Hello? . . . Oh, hi Principal Yang . . ."

My heart thundered in my chest. I tried to read Mom's expression, but she had a serious poker face on.

"We understand . . ." Mom continued. "No, we haven't seen it . . . I'm sure Dessa appreciates their support . . . Okay, I'll tell her. Thank you, Principal Yang . . . good-bye." She disconnected and dropped her phone back to the counter.

"Well?" Dad asked, setting the knife back on the counter.

"Coen Marsh's parents have declined to press charges," Mom said. "And after multiple calls and voicemails and e-mails from every member of the drama club this weekend, Principal Yang decided against expulsion."

I let out a long, relieved breath.

"She says you should be thankful to have such amazing friends," Mom continued. "She also wanted me to tell you she watched your video and will be extra vigilant when it comes to bullying."

"What video?" Dad asked.

"I'll show you later," I said. "Does that mean I'm not suspended anymore?" I crossed my fingers, waved them in front of me.

Mom shook her head. "Still ten days. *But*— Principal Yang did offer you one concession."

"What's that?"

"A ticket to tonight's final performance of *Romeo & Juliet*."

I nearly leapt off my stool. I wanted to hug Principal Yang so bad right now. But Mom was closer, and really more deserving, so I went over and wrapped my arms around her. "This is so great," I said. "I can't wait to tell Kat."

And I rushed off to my room, to find my phone among the mess and do just that.

ABOUT THE AUTHOR

Brandon Terrell is the author of numerous
books for young readers, including picture
books, novels, and graphic novels. He is also
one of the writers for *The Choo Choo Bob Show*,
an educational children's television program
about trains. When not hunched over his
laptop, Brandon enjoys watching movies and
television, reading, baseball, and spending
every spare moment with his wife and their
two children.